5/16

P9-CRE-119

Ben says Goodbye

Written by **Sarah Ellis**   Illustrated by **Kim La Fave**

pajamapress

First published in the United States in 2016
First published in Canada in 2015
Text copyright © 2015 Sarah Ellis
Illustrations copyright © 2015 Kim La Fave
This edition copyright © 2015 Pajama Press Inc.
This is a first edition.

10 9 8 7 6 5 4 3 2 1

www.pajamapress.ca   info@pajamapress.ca

Canada Council   Conseil des arts
for the Arts   du Canada

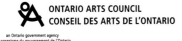   ONTARIO ARTS COUNCIL
CONSEIL DES ARTS DE L'ONTARIO    Canadä

an Ontario government agency
un organisme du gouvernement de l'Ontario

The publisher gratefully acknowledges the support of the Canada Council for the Arts and the Ontario Arts Council for its publishing program. We acknowledge the financial support of the Government of Canada through the Canada Book Fund (CBF) for our publishing activities.

Library and Archives Canada Cataloguing in Publication

Ellis, Sarah, author
    Ben says goodbye / written by Sarah Ellis ; illustrated by
Kim La Fave. – First edition.
    ISBN 978-1-927485-79-8 (bound)
    I. LaFave, Kim, illustrator II. Title.
PS8559.L57B46 2015   jC813'.54   C2015-
902333-5

Publisher Cataloging-in-Publication Data (U.S.)

Ellis, Sarah, 1952-
    Ben says goodbye / written by Sarah Ellis ; illustrated by Kim La Fave.

[32] pages : color illustrations ;   cm.

Summary: "When Ben's best friend moves away, he decides he will move, too - under the table, where he lives as Caveman Ben. Supported by his family, Ben is able to work through his feelings until he feels ready to reemerge and look forward to new friendships" – Provided by publisher.

ISBN-13: 978-1-927485-79-8

1. Friendship – Juvenile fiction. 2. Play – Juvenile fiction.
3. Emotions – Juvenile fiction. I. LaFave, Kim. II. Title.

[E]   dc23   PZ7.1.E565Be 2015

Cover and book design—Rebecca Buchanan

Manufactured by QuaLibre Inc./Print Plus
Printed in China

Pajama Press Inc.
181 Carlaw Ave. Suite 207 Toronto, Ontario Canada, M4M 2S1

Distributed in Canada by UTP Distribution
5201 Dufferin Street Toronto, Ontario Canada, M3H 5T8

Distributed in the U.S. by Ingram Publisher Services
1 Ingram Blvd. La Vergne, TN 37086, USA

For Elliott and Lochlan
—S.E.

For Julian and Zach
—K. La F.

Ben and Peter watched two strong movers put Peter's world into their big truck.

Box after box. **Box after box.** **Box after box.**

And then, not in a box, Peter's Red Lightning Bicycle.

Ben's father said, "Maybe Peter can come back to visit next summer."

Ben's sister Robin said, "I'll show you how to talk to Peter online."

Ben's brother Joe said,
"Want to play sniggle-ball?"

Ben's mother said, "It's time to say goodbye to Peter."

Ben did not want
to play sniggle-ball.
He did not want
to say goodbye to Peter.

Ben decided he would move too.
Not across the world. Not across
the country. Not across town.
He would move under the table.
He would become a caveboy.

Caveboy Ben slept on furs.
He ate with his fingers.
He played with rocks.
He protected himself with a club
and a pointed stick.
He tamed a lion for his only friend.

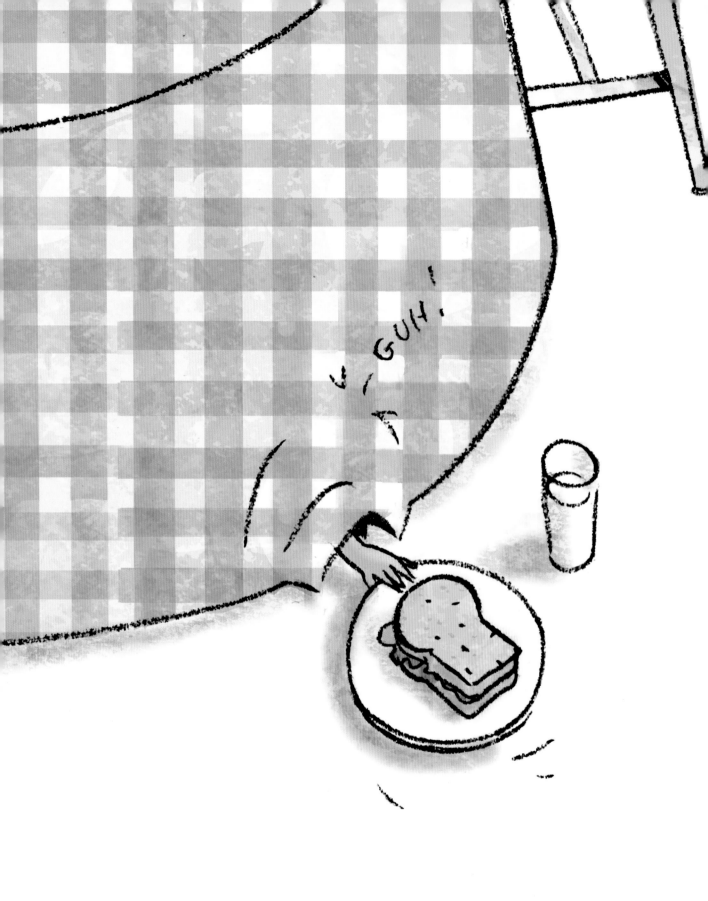

Caveboy Ben did not brush his teeth
or say please and thank-you.
He only said, "Guh." He said "guh"
for yes and "guh" for no and "guh"
for go away.

High on the walls of his cave he drew with his
pointed stick. He drew the story of two boys
who were best friends. He drew how they
flew on magic wings and beat the bad guys.
He drew how they ran faster than race cars
and talked silly talk and saved sad animals
and fooled big kids.

Caveboy Ben drew the story of
two faraway friends who each
dug a hole in his backyard.
They dug past dirt and rocks,
roots and worms, sewer pipes
and subway lines, ancient cities
and buried pirate treasure.

They dug until they met right at the center of the Earth, in the place where rocks melt. It was a good place for a barbecue.

So the two boys
ate chili dogs and
played sniggle-ball.

Then they went home,
each to his own side
of the world.

When the walls of the cave were completely covered, Caveboy Ben smelled butter.

He crawled out.

There was a fire in the fireplace.
The whole family was crowded
onto the couch.

Mom and Dad squished sideways and made a little cave for Ben.

"Comfy?" said Mom.
"Popcorn?" said Robin.
"Guh," said Ben.

From across the street came a loud beeping sound. Ben knelt on the couch to look. A big truck was backing into the driveway. Two strong movers got out. They pushed up the back door of the truck.

Box after box.

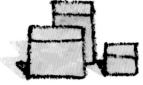

Box after box.

Box after box.

TOYS

FRAGILE

THIS
END
UP

UP →

T J
BOOKS

And then, not in
a box, a Scorcher
Scooter in neon blue.
Just the right size for
a new friend.